Eb Alto Saxophone

Tradition of Excellence™

TECHNIQUE & MUSICIANSHIP

for group or private instruction

by Bruce Pearson and Ryan Nowlin

Welcome to *Tradition of Excellence™: Technique & Musicianship*! Developing technical skill and artistic sensitivity on your instrument is an essential step toward becoming a well-rounded musician. The exercises in this book will help your progress—even scales can be played musically! Of particular importance are the *Musicianship Tips* shown on exercise 8 of each key study. They offer valuable advice and should be applied to the subsequent exercise, as well as the music you play outside of these lessons.

Table of Contents

ISBN 10: 0-8497-7181-1 • ISBN 13: 978-0-8497-7181-1

©2012 Kjos Music Press, Neil A. Kjos Music Company, Distributor, 4382 Jutland Drive, San Diego, California, 92117.
International copyright secured. All rights reserved. Printed in U.S.A.

1. Slurs and Lip Slurs

1. Slurs and Lip Slurs can be played
simultaneously with **1. Technique Builder**.

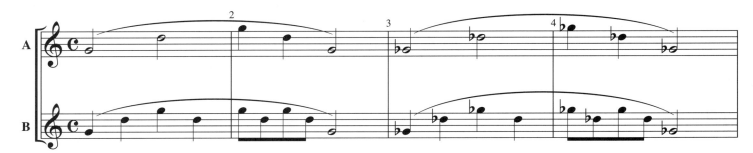

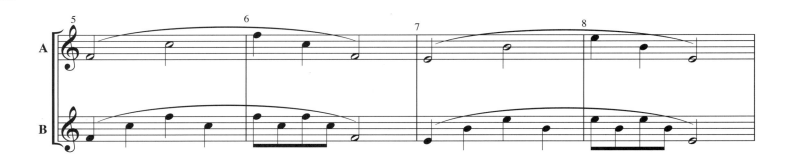

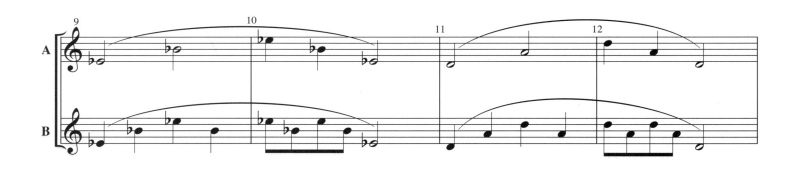

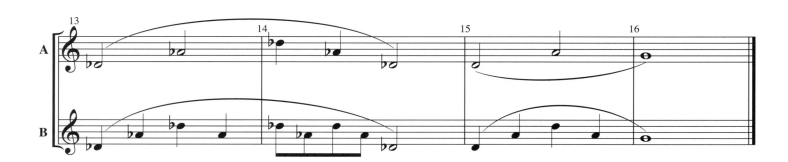

1. Technique Builder

2. Slurs and Lip Slurs

2. Slurs and Lip Slurs can be played simultaneously with **2. Technique Builder**.

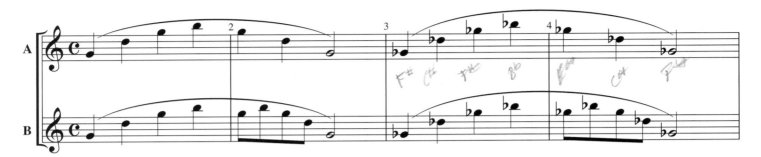

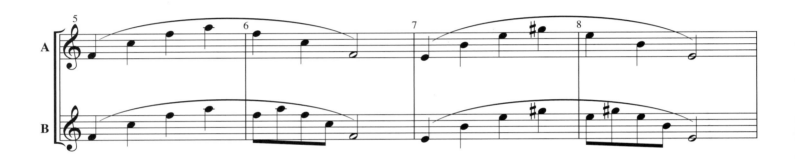

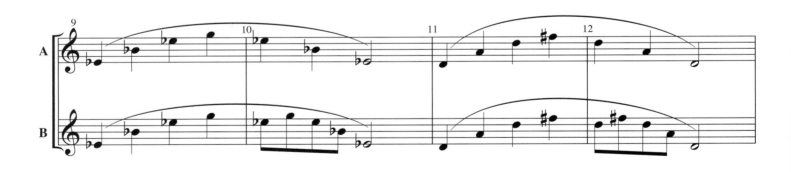

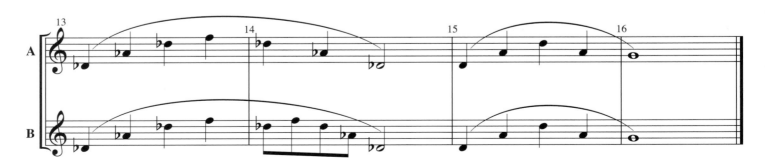

2. Technique Builder

3. Slurs and Lip Slurs

3. Slurs and Lip Slurs can be played simultaneously with **3. Technique Builder**.

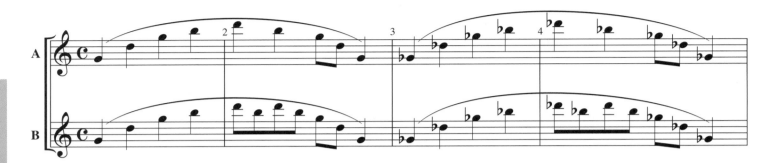

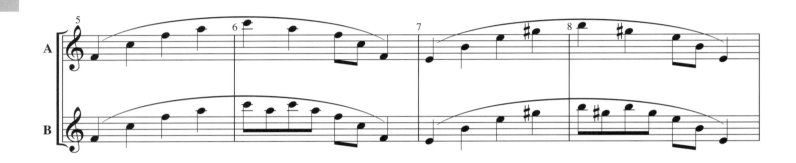

3. Technique Builder

4. Match and Pass That Note

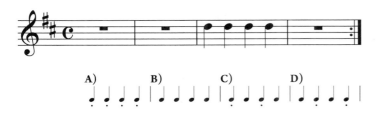

5. Dynamic Control

W64XE

1. G Major Scale (Concert B♭ Major)

2. Thirds

3. Arpeggios [I–IV–I–V^7–I] and Chords [I–IV–I–V^7–I]

4. Articulation and Technique Etude #1

Basic ♩ = 80; Advanced ♩ = 92; Mastery ♩ = 120

5. Articulation and Technique Etude #2

Basic ♩. = 80; Advanced ♩. = 92; Mastery ♩. = 120

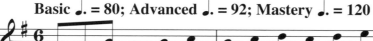

6. Articulation and Technique Etude #3

Basic ♩ = 72; Advanced ♩ = 84; Mastery ♩ = 100

7. Interval and Tuning Etude

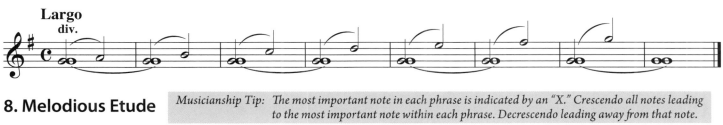

8. Melodious Etude

Musicianship Tip: The most important note in each phrase is indicated by an "X." Crescendo all notes leading to the most important note within each phrase. Decrescendo leading away from that note.

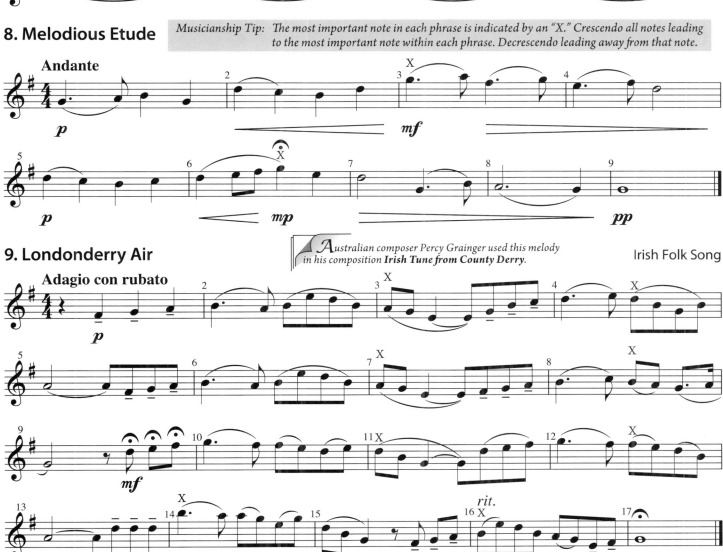

9. Londonderry Air

Irish Folk Song

*Australian composer Percy Grainger used this melody in his composition **Irish Tune from County Derry**.*

10. Chorale — Band Arrangement

Martin Luther (1483–1546)
German Composer
arr. Ryan Nowlin

E Minor Studies (Concert G Minor)

1. E Natural Minor Scale (Concert G Minor)

2. E Harmonic Minor Scale (Concert G Minor)

3. E Melodic Minor Scale (Concert G Minor)

4. Arpeggios [i–iv–i–V^7–i] and Chords [i–iv–i–V^7–i]

5. Articulation and Technique Etude #1

Basic ♩ = 80; Advanced ♩ = 92; Mastery ♩ = 120

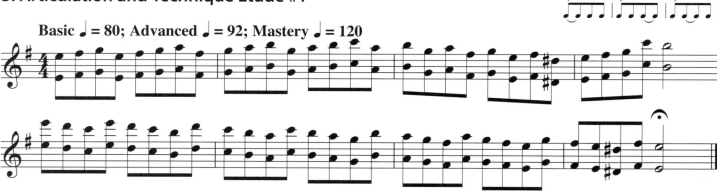

6. Articulation and Technique Etude #2

Basic ♩ = 80; Advanced ♩ = 92; Mastery ♩ = 120

7. Interval and Tuning Etude

8. Melodious Etude

Musicianship Tip: Pay close attention to the staccato quarter notes while rehearsing this exercise. Good bands start notes together. GREAT bands also end notes together.

9. Minuet

Henry Purcell (1659–1695)
English Composer

10. Chorale — Band Arrangement

Bach adapted many popular hymns of his day for use in his own compositions.

Hans Leo Hassler (1564–1612)
harmonized by J.S. Bach (1685–1750)
arr. Ryan Nowlin

1. C Major Scale (Concert E♭ Major)

2. Thirds

3. Arpeggios [I–IV–I–V7–I] and Chords [I–IV–I–V7–I]

4. Articulation and Technique Etude #1

Basic ♩ = 80; Advanced ♩ = 92; Mastery ♩ = 120

5. Articulation and Technique Etude #2

Basic ♩. = 80; Advanced ♩. = 92; Mastery ♩. = 120

6. Articulation and Technique Etude #3

Basic ♩ = 72; Advanced ♩ = 84; Mastery ♩ = 100

7. Interval and Tuning Etude

8. Melodious Etude

Musicianship Tip: When playing in ¾ time, the first note of each measure is often played slightly louder within the shape of each phrase.

9. Intermezzo Sinfonico (from Cavalleria Rusticana)

Cavalleria Rusticana won first prize in a composition contest and the composer became an instant success.

Pietro Mascagni
(1863–1945)
Italian Composer

10. Chorale — Band Arrangement

Johann Crüger (1598–1662)
German Composer
arr. Ryan Nowlin

1. A Natural Minor Scale (Concert C Minor)

2. A Harmonic Minor Scale (Concert C Minor)

3. A Melodic Minor Scale (Concert C Minor)

4. Arpeggios [i–iv–i–V7–i] and Chords [i–iv–i–V^7–i]

5. Articulation and Technique Etude #1

Basic ♩ = 80; Advanced ♩ = 92; Mastery ♩ = 120

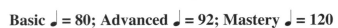

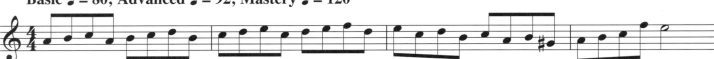

6. Articulation and Technique Etude #2

Basic ♩ = 80; Advanced ♩ = 92; Mastery ♩ = 120

7. Interval and Tuning Etude

8. Melodious Etude

Musicianship Tip: When playing in a cantabile or singing style, the last note of a slur should be held for its full value.

9. Ständchen (from Schwanengesang)

Ständchen means "serenade." In this song, the singer begs his love to return his feelings. The tempo marking is pronounced "maessick." The letter in the middle is called "eszett" or "double s."

Franz Schubert (1797–1828) Austrian Composer

10. Chorale — Band Arrangement

Johann Crüger (1598–1662) German Composer arr. Ryan Nowlin

1. D Major Scale (Concert F Major)

2. Thirds

3. Arpeggios [I–IV–I–V^7–I] and Chords [I–IV–I–V^7–I]

4. Articulation and Technique Etude #1

Basic ♩ = 80; **Advanced** ♩ = 92; **Mastery** ♩ = 120

5. Articulation and Technique Etude #2

Basic ♩. = 80; **Advanced** ♩. = 92; **Mastery** ♩. = 120

6. Articulation and Technique Etude #3

Basic ♩ = 72; **Advanced** ♩ = 84; **Mastery** ♩ = 100

7. Interval and Tuning Etude

8. Melodious Etude

> *Musicianship Tip: Shorter notes tend to naturally lead to longer notes. To assist this motion, give the shorter notes a slight "lift."*

9. Nocturne
(from A Midsummer Night's Dream)

This music was written for a production of Shakespeare's play at the request of King William IV of Prussia.

Felix Mendelssohn (1809–1847)
German Composer

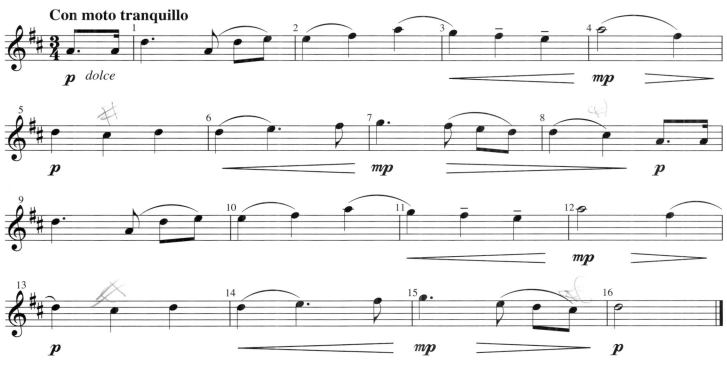

10. Chorale — Band Arrangement

from Stralsund Gesangbuch (1665)
arr. Ryan Nowlin

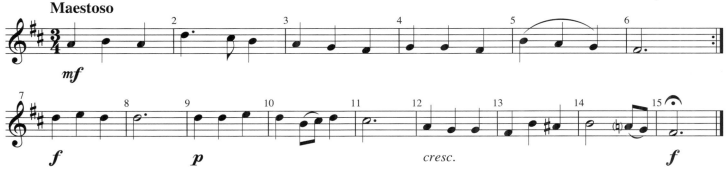

1. B Natural Minor Scale (Concert D Minor)

2. B Harmonic Minor Scale (Concert D Minor)

3. B Melodic Minor Scale (Concert D Minor)

4. Arpeggios [i–iv–i–V^7–i] and Chords [i–iv–i–V^7–i]

5. Articulation and Technique Etude #1

Basic ♩ = 80; Advanced ♩ = 92; Mastery ♩ = 120

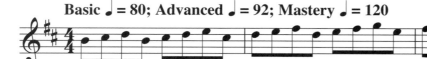

6. Articulation and Technique Etude #2

Basic ♩ = 80; Advanced ♩ = 92; Mastery ♩ = 120

7. Interval and Tuning Etude

Musicianship Tip: Shorter ascending notes (as in measure 4, beats 2 & 3) create movement. Give these notes a slight crescendo.

8. Melodious Etude

9. Theme from Swan Lake

This ballet was premiered in Moscow on March 4, 1876.

Peter Ilyich Tchaikovsky (1840–1893)
Russian Composer

10. Chorale — Band Arrangement

Traditional French Melody
harmonized by Ralph Vaughn Williams (1906)
arr. Ryan Nowlin

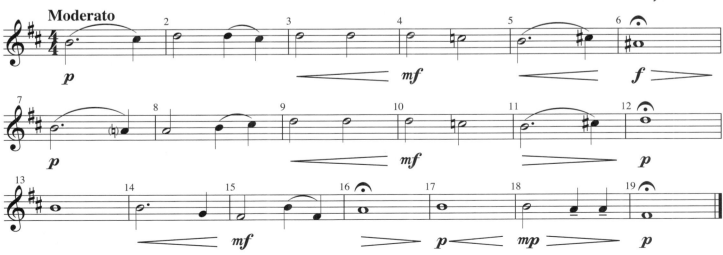

1. F Major Scale (Concert A♭ Major)

2. Thirds

3. Arpeggios [I–IV–I–V⁷–I] and Chords [I–IV–I–V⁷–I]

4. Articulation and Technique Etude #1

Basic ♩ = 80; Advanced ♩ = 92; Mastery ♩ = 120

5. Articulation and Technique Etude #2

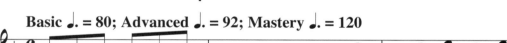

Basic ♩. = 80; Advanced ♩. = 92; Mastery ♩. = 120

6. Articulation and Technique Etude #3

Basic ♩ = 72; Advanced ♩ = 84; Mastery ♩ = 100

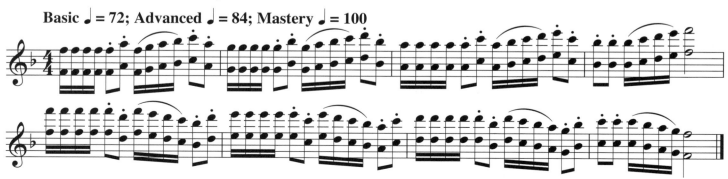

7. Interval and Tuning Etude

Largo

8. Melodious Etude

Moderato

Musicianship Tip: When two notes are slurred, the first note is often played with more weight and is tapered, giving the second note less volume than the first.

9. Minuet

Andante grazioso

Leopold was Wolfgang Amadeus Mozart's father.

Leopold Mozart (1719–1787)
Austrian Composer

10. Chorale — Band Arrangement

Philip Bliss (1838–1876)
American Composer
arr. Ryan Nowlin

Andante

1. D Natural Minor Scale (Concert F Minor)

2. D Harmonic Minor Scale (Concert F Minor)

3. D Melodic Minor Scale (Concert F Minor)

4. Arpeggios [i–iv–i–V⁷–i] and Chords [i–iv–i–V⁷–i]

5. Articulation and Technique Etude #1

Basic ♩ = 80; Advanced ♩ = 92; Mastery ♩ = 120

6. Articulation and Technique Etude #2

Basic ♩ = 80; Advanced ♩ = 92; Mastery ♩ = 120

7. Interval and Tuning Etude

8. Melodious Etude

Musicianship Tip: *An anacrusis (pickup note) in a cantabile (singing) style is often played tenuto and slightly stressed.*

9. Greensleeves

*The earliest known source of this song dates back to 1580. Shakespeare mentioned **Greensleeves** in his play "The Merry Wives of Windsor," which indicates that the song became very popular.*

English Folk Song

10. Chorale — Band Arrangement

Georg Neumark (1621–1681)
German Composer
arr. Ryan Nowlin

1. Bb Major Scale (Concert Db Major)

2. Thirds

3. Arpeggios [I–IV–I–V^7–I] and Chords [I–IV–I–V^7–I]

4. Articulation and Technique Etude #1

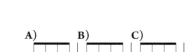

Basic ♩ = 80; Advanced ♩ = 92; Mastery ♩ = 120

5. Articulation and Technique Etude #2

Basic ♩. = 80; Advanced ♩. = 92; Mastery ♩. = 120

6. Articulation and Technique Etude #3

Basic ♩ = 72; Advanced ♩ = 84; Mastery ♩ = 100

7. Interval and Tuning Etude

Largo
div.

8. Melodious Etude

> *Musicianship Tip:* The note preceding a syncopated note should be played shorter and slightly softer than the syncopated note. The syncopated note should be played full length and slightly louder than the notes surrounding it.

Modéré *[Moderately]*

mf stacc.   *p cresc.*   *f*   *mf*

9. Ecossaise

> *In addition to his nine famous symphonies, Beethoven wrote many charming dances, like this ecossaise (Scottish dance).*

Ludwig van Beethoven (1770–1827)
German Composer

Allegro

mf stacc.   *f*

f

10. Chorale — Band Arrangement

Netherlands Hymn
arr. Ryan Nowlin

Moderato

p   *mp*   *p cresc.*   *mf*   *p*   *mp*   *p cresc.*   *mf*   *p*

1. G Natural Minor Scale (Concert B♭ Minor)

2. G Harmonic Minor Scale (Concert B♭ Minor)

3. G Melodic Minor Scale (Concert B♭ Minor)

4. Arpeggios [i–iv–i–V^7–i] and Chords [i–iv–i–V^7–i]

5. Articulation and Technique Etude #1

Basic ♩ = 80; Advanced ♩ = 92; Mastery ♩ = 120

6. Articulation and Technique Etude #2

Basic ♩ = 80; Advanced ♩ = 92; Mastery ♩ = 120

7. Interval and Tuning Etude

Largo
div.

8. Melodious Etude

> **Musicianship Tip:** When playing dotted eighth and sixteenth note rhythms, the sixteenth note tends to lead to the following dotted eighth note. Assist this motion by giving the sixteenth note a slight "lift." Avoid a triplet feel.

Assez vite *[Allegretto]*

mf

9. Prèlude (from L'Arlésienne)

> *Bizet uses this theme throughout his music for the play "L'Arlésienne" [The Girl from Arles]. Most notably, this theme recurs in the famous "Farandole" when violence breaks out during a community dance.*

Georges Bizet (1838–1875)
French Composer

Allegro vivo e deciso

f

10. Chorale — Band Arrangement

Joseph Parry (1841–1903)
Welsh Composer
arr. Ryan Nowlin

Allegretto

1. A Major Scale (Concert C Major)

2. Thirds

3. Arpeggios [I–IV–I–V⁷–I] and Chords [I–IV–I–V⁷–I]

4. Articulation and Technique Etude #1

Basic ♩ = 80; Advanced ♩ = 92; Mastery ♩ = 120

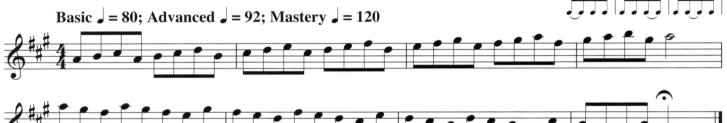

5. Articulation and Technique Etude #2

Basic ♩. = 80; Advanced ♩. = 92; Mastery ♩. = 120

6. Articulation and Technique Etude #3

Basic ♩ = 72; Advanced ♩ = 84; Mastery ♩ = 100

7. Interval and Tuning Etude

Largo

8. Melodious Etude

Musicianship Tip: To create motion, crescendo longer notes at the beginning of a phrase, especially if they are followed by shorter notes.

Allegretto

9. Ave Maria

Franz Schubert (1797–1828)
Austrian Composer

Sehr langsam *[Very slow]*

10. Chorale — Band Arrangement

This chorale is also known as the "Navy Hymn" and is regularly sung at the U.S. Naval Academy in Annapolis, Maryland.

John Bacchus Dykes (1823–1876)
American Composer
arr. Ryan Nowlin

Moderately

W64XE

1. F# Natural Minor Scale (Concert A Minor)

2. F# Harmonic Minor Scale (Concert A Minor)

3. F# Melodic Minor Scale (Concert A Minor)

4. Arpeggios [i–iv–i–V^7–i] and Chords [i–iv–i–V^7–i]

5. Articulation and Technique Etude #1

Basic ♩ = 80; Advanced ♩ = 92; Mastery ♩ = 120

6. Articulation and Technique Etude #2

Basic ♩ = 80; Advanced ♩ = 92; Mastery ♩ = 120

W64XE

7. Interval and Tuning Etude

8. Melodious Etude

Musicianship Tip: When a dotted eighth/sixteenth note rhythm is under a slur, give the sixteenth note more weight and length.

9. Pavane

Fauré was a renowned teacher in Paris. Famous composers, including Maurice Ravel, were among his students.

Gabriel Fauré (1845–1924)
French Composer

10. Chorale — Band Arrangement

American Spiritual
arr. Ryan Nowlin

1. E Major Scale (Concert G Major)

2. Thirds

3. Arpeggios [I–IV–I–V⁷–I] and Chords [I–IV–I–V⁷–I]

4. Articulation and Technique Etude #1

Basic ♩ = 80; Advanced ♩ = 92; Mastery ♩ = 120

5. Articulation and Technique Etude #2

Basic ♩. = 80; Advanced ♩. = 92; Mastery ♩. = 120

6. Articulation and Technique Etude #3

Basic ♩ = 72; Advanced ♩ = 84; Mastery ♩ = 100

7. Interval and Tuning Etude

Largo

div.

8. Melodious Etude

Musicianship Tip: Increase musical tension through the use of a crescendo and create greater anticipation by delaying the climax of a phrase through the use of a ritardando (rit.).

Andante

Fine

D.C. al Fine

9. Simple Gifts

Simple Gifts gained popularity when the American composer Aaron Copland used it in his 1944 ballet "Appalachian Spring."

Joseph Brackett (1797–1882)
American Composer

Tenderly

poco rit.

a tempo

Più mosso

rit.

meno mosso

10. Chorale — Band Arrangement

Henry F. Hemy (1818–1888)
Australian Composer
arr. Ryan Nowlin

Maestoso

W64XE

1. C# Natural Minor Scale (Concert E Minor)

2. C# Harmonic Minor Scale (Concert E Minor)

3. C# Melodic Minor Scale (Concert E Minor)

4. Arpeggios [i–iv–i–V⁷–i] and Chords [i–iv–i–V⁷–i]

5. Articulation and Technique Etude #1

Basic ♩ = 80; Advanced ♩ = 92; Mastery ♩ = 120

6. Articulation and Technique Etude #2

Basic ♩ = 80; Advanced ♩ = 92; Mastery ♩ = 120

W64XE

7. Interval and Tuning Etude

Largo
div.

8. Melodious Etude

> **Musicianship Tip:** *The first note of a slur is often held slightly longer than the subsequent notes within the slur.*

Moderato

9. Plainsong

> *Plainsong is related to Gregorian Chant, with examples dating back to the 3rd century. Because many plainsong melodies pre-date modern musical notation and the invention of measures, rhythm is historically performed less strictly in plainsong than in other musical styles.*

Traditional

Andante con rubato

10. Chorale — Band Arrangement

Traditional Hebrew Melody
Adaptation: Meyer Lyon (1750–1797)
arr. Ryan Nowlin

Andante

1. B Major Scale (Concert D Major)

2. Thirds

3. Arpeggios [I–IV–I–V⁷–I] and Chords [I–IV–I–V⁷–I]

4. Articulation and Technique Etude #1

Basic ♩ = 80; Advanced ♩ = 92; Mastery ♩ = 120

5. Articulation and Technique Etude #2

Basic ♩. = 80; Advanced ♩. = 92; Mastery ♩. = 120

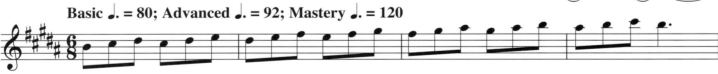

6. Articulation and Technique Etude #3

Basic ♩ = 72; Advanced ♩ = 84; Mastery ♩ = 100

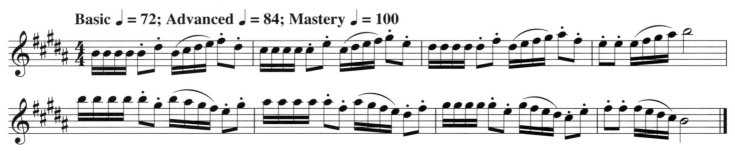

7. Interval and Tuning Etude

8. Melodious Etude

Musicianship Tip: Lower-pitched notes tend to lead to higher-pitched notes, while higher-pitched notes tend to lead to lower-pitched notes. Assist this movement by applying crescendos and decrescendos.

9. Shenandoah

The origins of this song are unclear. Many different versions are popular today. One version expresses longing for the Shenandoah Valley in Virginia, while another professes love for the daughter of an American Indian chief.

American Folk Song

10. Chorale — Band Arrangement

Samuel S. Wesley (1810–1876)
English Composer
arr. Ryan Nowlin

1. G# Natural Minor Scale (Concert B Minor)

2. G# Harmonic Minor Scale (Concert B Minor)

3. G# Melodic Minor Scale (Concert B Minor)

4. Arpeggios [i–iv–i–V⁷–i] and Chords [i–iv–i–V⁷–i]

5. Articulation and Technique Etude #1

Basic ♩ = 80; Advanced ♩ = 92; Mastery ♩ = 120

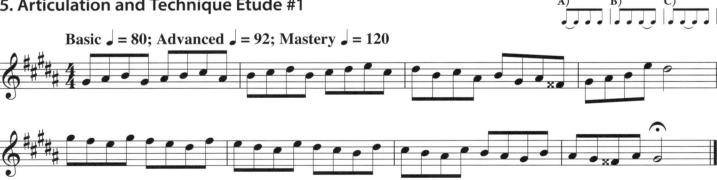

6. Articulation and Technique Etude #2

Basic ♩ = 80; Advanced ♩ = 92; Mastery ♩ = 120

7. Interval and Tuning Etude

8. Melodious Etude

Musicianship Tip: Create a sense of repose on longer notes that follow shorter notes (as in measure 2) by applying a slight decrescendo.

9. Torna a Surriento

Elvis Presley's 1961 number one hit "Surrender" is based on this melody.

Ernesto de Curtis (1875–1937)
Italian Composer

10. Chorale — Band Arrangement

English Folk Song
arr. Ryan Nowlin

W64XE

To play with excellent intonation is a goal of every individual musician and musical ensemble. The art of playing in tune is an ongoing process based on the necessary prerequisites of excellent tone quality and skilled listening. Without either of these components, efforts to play in tune will fall short.

The most important component for playing in tune on the saxophone is a good tone quality. In fact, you can't tune a poor tone. Another component for playing in tune is having a properly adjusted instrument and reed. Intonation is also dramatically affected by temperature. Warm temperatures cause saxophones to play sharp; cold temperatures cause them to play flat. It is important for saxophonists to be aware of (and adjust for) temperature differences.

Saxophone manufacturers make their saxophones to play in tune at A440. Playing in tune is a task that requires mechanical and physical adjustments as well as knowledge of the pitch tendencies of one's own instrument. To begin the tuning process, push the mouthpiece mid-way onto the cork and play the following two exercises:

Using an electronic tuner, determine if you are playing the F# flat, sharp, or in tune. If the note is sharp, the mouthpiece should be pulled out to cause the pitch to sound flatter. If the note is flat, push the mouthpiece further onto the cork.

The following notes are naturally out of tune on most saxophones:

Tendency to be flat: Tendency to be sharp:

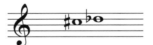   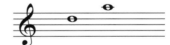

Using an electronic tuner, check each note on your saxophone and mark the pitch tendency of each note on the fingering chart on the inside back cover using a + for sharp and a – for flat.

From **Teaching Band with Excellence** (W74), ©2011 Kjos Music Press. Used with permission.

1. Tone, Balance, and Tuning

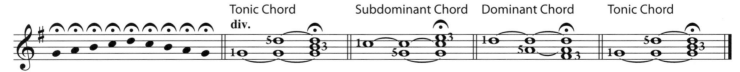

2. C (Concert E♭) Tuning Chord

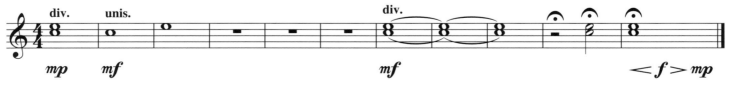

1. G Major Chorale (Concert B♭)

William Croft (1678–1727)
English Composer
arr. Bruce Pearson

2. D Major Chorale (Concert F)

Johann Sebastian Bach (1685–1750)
German Composer
arr. Bruce Pearson

The **Circle of Fourths** (also called the **Circle of Fifths**) is a tool showing the relationship between major and minor keys. Moving *clockwise* around the circle, each key name is the same as the fourth scale degree of the key before it. For example, if you begin with the key of C Major and move one key *clockwise* along the circle, you reach the key of F Major. The note F is the *fourth* scale degree of the key of C Major, therefore the key of F Major is a "fourth" apart from the key of C Major. This pattern continues around the circle (going clockwise), giving the circle of fourths its name. (If you travel *counterclockwise* around the circle, each key name is the same as the *fifth* scale degree of the key before it, so the circle can also be called the circle of fifths.)

The circle of fourths also organizes the key signatures by the number of sharps or flats in each key. Traveling *clockwise* from the key of C Major, each key signature adds one flat, up to seven flats (one for each letter of the musical alphabet). The flats are added in the *order of flats:* B, E, A, D, G, C, F. Traveling *counterclockwise* (along the circle of fifths) from the key of C Major, each key signature adds one sharp, up to seven sharps. The sharps are added in the *order of sharps:* F, C, G, D, A, E, B.

A note regarding the bottom of the circle (enharmonic keys): Just as enharmonic pitches (such as B and C♭) have two names for the same sound, enharmonic keys include identical sets of pitches but name each pitch differently. These enharmonic key pairs include B (5♯s) and C♭ (7♭s), F♯ (6♯s) and G♭ (6♭s), and C♯ (7♯s) and D♭ (5♭s).

The names of major keys are indicated by circles.
The names of minor keys are indicated by rectangles.

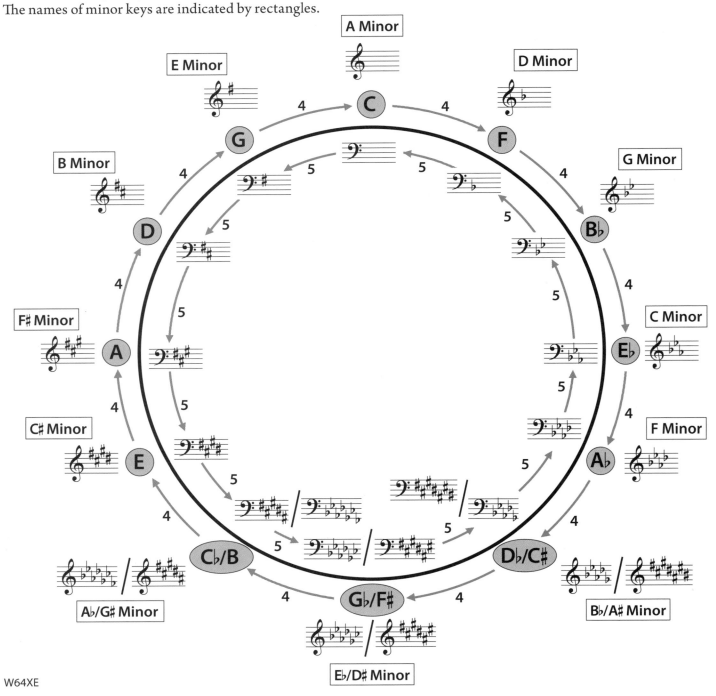

1. D Major Scale (Concert F)

2. G Major Scale (Concert B♭)

3. C Major Scale (Concert E♭)

4. F Major Scale (Concert A♭)

5. B♭ Major Scale (Concert D♭/C♯)

6. E♭ Major Scale (Concert G♭/F♯)

7. A♭ Major Scale (Concert C♭/B)

8. D♭/C♯ Major Scale (Concert E)

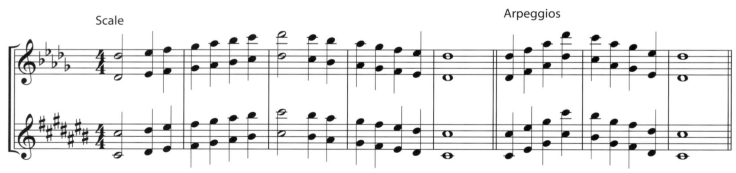

9. G♭/F♯ Major Scale (Concert A)

10. C♭/B Major Scale (Concert D)

11. E Major Scale (Concert G)

12. A Major Scale (Concert C)

1. B Minor Scale (Concert D)

2. E Minor Scale (Concert G)

3. A Minor Scale (Concert C)

4. D Minor Scale (Concert F)

5. G Minor Scale (Concert Bb/A#)

6. C Minor Scale (Concert E♭/D♯)

7. F Minor Scale (Concert A♭/G♯)

8. B♭/A♯ Minor Scale (Concert C♯)

9. E♭/D♯ Minor Scale (Concert F♯)

Scale (Melodic)   Arpeggios

Thirds

10. A♭/G♯ Minor Scale (Concert B)

Scale (Melodic)   Arpeggios

Thirds

11. C♯ Minor Scale (Concert E)

Scale (Melodic)   Arpeggios

Thirds

12. F♯ Minor Scale (Concert A)

Scale (Melodic)   Arpeggios

Thirds

C *or* **4/4**

1.

11.

2.

12.

3.

13.

4.

14.

5.

15.

6.
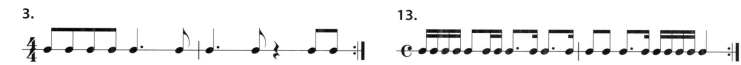

16.

7.

17.

8.

18.

9.
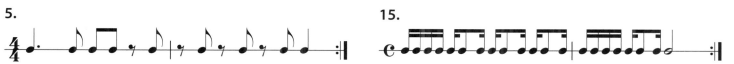

19.

10.

20.
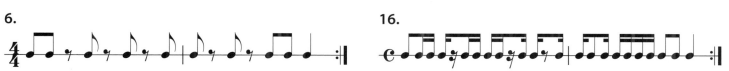

$\frac{3}{4}$

21.

31.

22.

32.

23.

33.

24.

34.

25.

35.

26.

36.

27.

37.

28.

38.

29.

39.

30.

40.

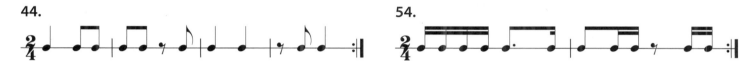

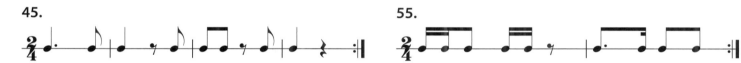

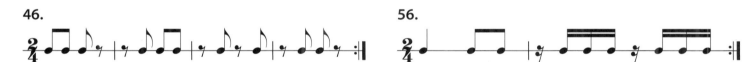

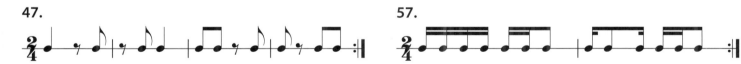

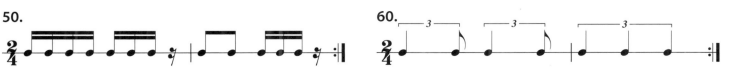

¢ *or* **2/2**

61.

71.

62.

72.

63.

73.

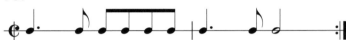

64.

74.

65.

75.

66.

76.

67.

77.

68.

78.

69.

79.

70.

80.

$\frac{9}{8}$

101.

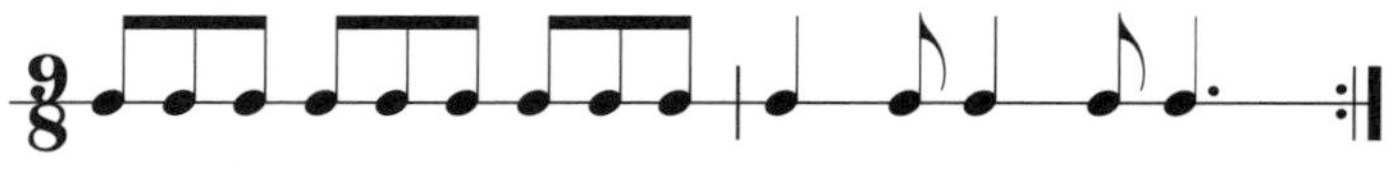

102.

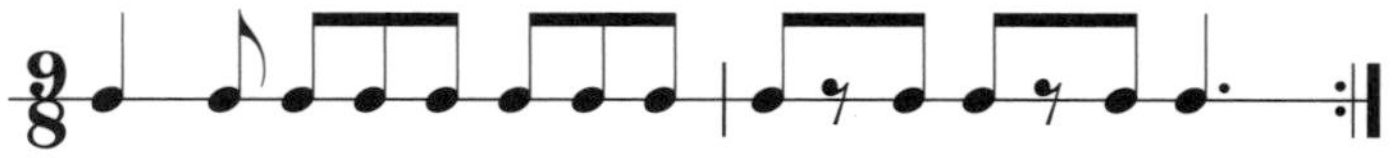

103.

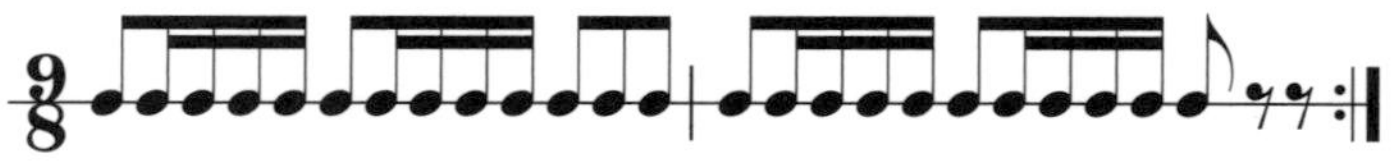

104.

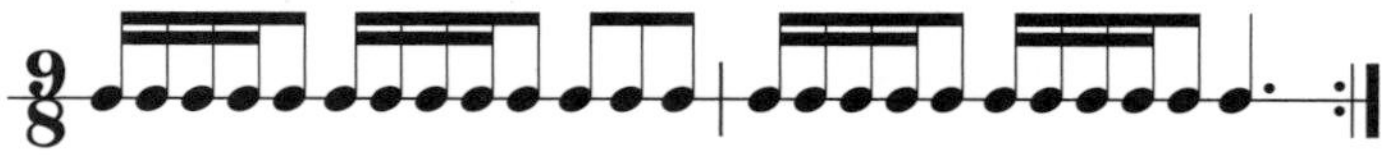

105.

106.

107.

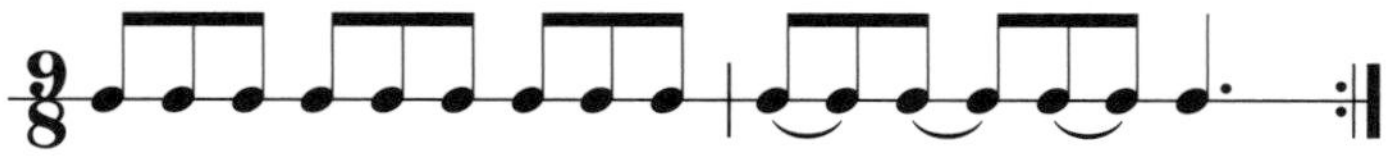

108.

109.

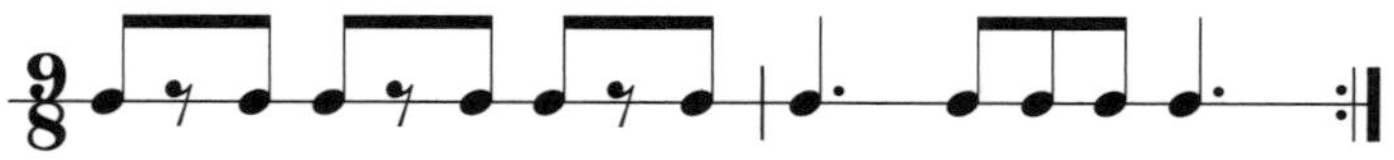

110.

$\frac{12}{8}$

111.

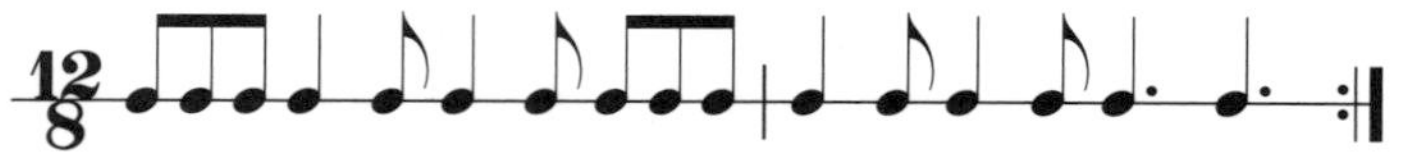

112.

113.

114.

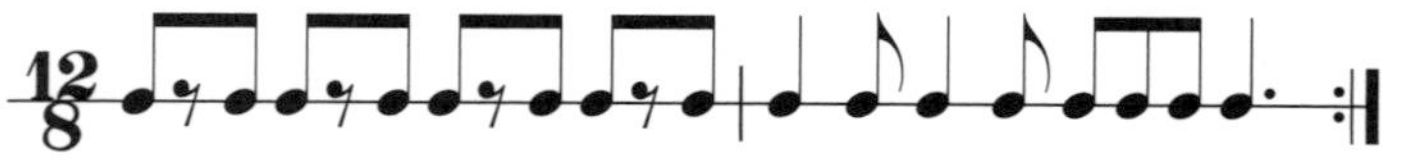

115.

116.

117.

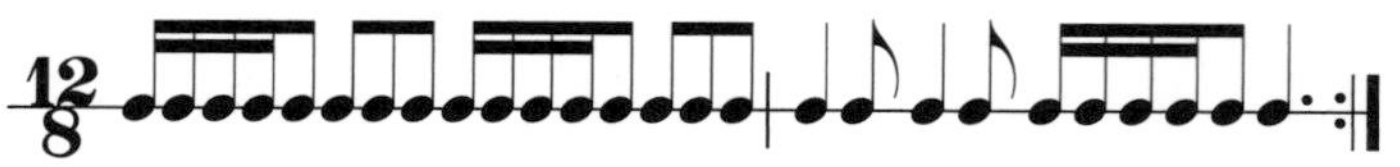

118.

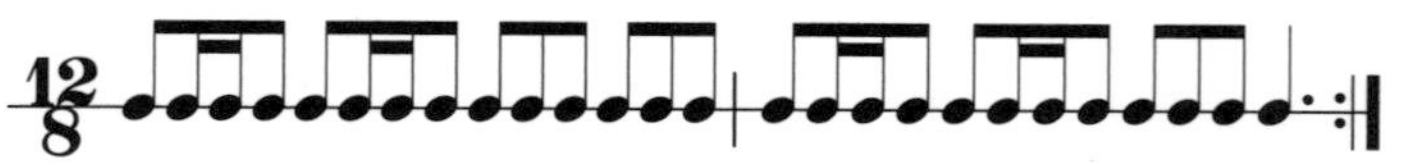

119.

120.

O = open

● = pressed down

Move the gray key rapidly to produce the trill.

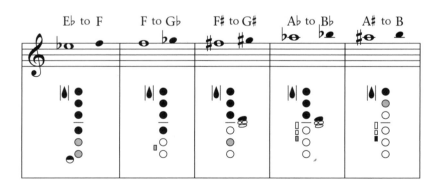
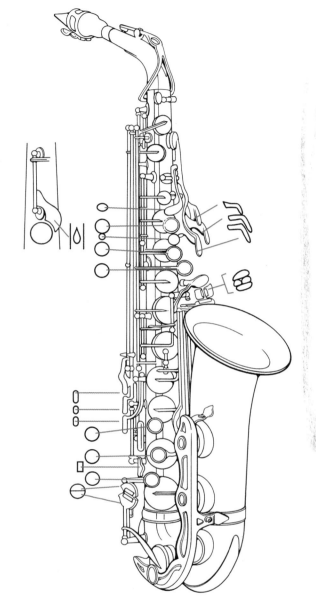